NO ROOM
FOR A
PUP!

TO PETER, JACK AND CALVIN, WITH LOVE! — L.M.
TO MY FIRST AND FOREVER PUPPY LOVE, E.J., A PINT-SIZED PUP — E.S.

Text © 2019 Elizabeth Suneby and Laurel Molk
Illustrations © 2019 Laurel Molk

Kids Can Press gratefully acknowledges the financial support of the Government
of Ontario, through Ontario Creates, for our publishing activity.

Published in Canada and the U.S. by Kids Can Press Ltd.
25 Dockside Drive, Toronto, ON M5A 0B5

Kids Can Press is a Corus Entertainment Inc. company

www.kidscanpress.com

The artwork in this book was created with watercolor, pencil, bits of paper,
tea bags, other sundry items and a dash of Photoshop.
The text is set in Wilke.

OCT 1 5 2019   Edited by Debbie Rogosin
Designed by Andrew Dupuis

Printed and bound in Malaysia in 3/2019 by Tien Wah Press (Pte) Ltd.

CM 19 0 9 8 7 6 5 4 3 2 1

Library and Archives Canada Cataloguing in Publication

Suneby, Elizabeth, 1958–, author
No room for a pup! / written by Elizabeth Suneby and Laurel Molk;
illustrated by Laurel Molk.

ISBN 978-1-5253-0029-5 (hardcover)

I. Molk, Laurel, author, illustrator II. Title.

PZ7.S9145No 2019   j813'.6   C2018-906344-0

Kids Can Press

ADOPT A PET!

No Room for a Pup! is a
thoroughly modern twist
on a venerable Yiddish
folktale that highlights the
importance of gratitude
for what one already has.
The story was popularized
in Margot Zemach's 1978
Caldecott Honor book, *It
Could Always Be Worse.*

No Room for a Pup!

By Elizabeth Suneby and Laurel Molk

Pictures by Laurel Molk

Mia lived with her mom in a very small apartment in a very big city. She wanted a dog more than anything. But every time Mia asked, her mom always said the same thing: "There's just NO ROOM. Not even for one pint-sized pup."

Mia thought there was plenty of
room for a puppy. It wasn't like she
was asking for an elephant.

Every morning before school, Mia went down the hall to her grandma's apartment for breakfast.

One morning, Mia spied a sign in the elevator. "Puppies to good homes! Apartment 202." Her eyes lit up. "That's where your friend Alina lives. Can we go see them?"

"After school," promised Grandma. "But remember, we're only visiting."

Mia loved ALL the puppies. Especially the one that climbed into her lap.

"I wish Mom would let me have a puppy," Mia sighed. "My teacher says there's always room for one more. Besides, Spot is so tiny we could fit ten of him." Mia smiled as she imagined ten little puppies running around her apartment.

"Wait a second, Grandma — I have a great idea!"

Grandma liked Mia's plan
and called a few friends ...

The next morning, the doorbell buzzed.
It was Grandma, with her pet parrot.
"I'm having my place painted, so Mia and
I will eat breakfast here. And I'll spend the
night. You'll hardly notice me or Roger."

"Oh no, not Roger!" groaned Mom.
"Roger, Roger!" squawked the parrot.

After school, Mia and Grandma came home
with the class rabbit.

"I told my teacher I'd take Sprinkles today,"
said Mia. "It's Sophie's turn tomorrow."

Mom rolled her eyes. "There's just NO ROOM.
Not even for one itty bitty bunny!"

"Bitty bunny, bitty bunny!"
squawked the parrot.
    The rabbit zipped and zoomed
around the room.

Then the doorbell buzzed. It was Grandma's neighbor. "Thanks for taking care of Tigger!" he called as he dashed down the hall.

Mom threw up her hands. "There's just NO ROOM,"
she wailed. "Not even for one pretty kitty!"

"Pretty kitty, pretty kitty!" squawked the parrot.
The cat chased the rabbit that zipped and zoomed
around the room.

Grandma's phone rang. "It's Mrs. McGillicuddy.
She needs me to look after Pierre."
Within minutes, a dog appeared at the door.

Mom shook her head. "There's just NO ROOM,"
she cried. "Not even for one doggone dog!"
"Doggone dog, doggone dog!" squawked the parrot.
The dog dashed up, down and all around. The cat
chased the rabbit that zipped and zoomed around
the room.

With all the houseguests,
no one got much sleep.

The next morning the doorbell buzzed again,
and in crowded Grandma's book club.

One lady even brought her pet pig.

It was bedlam. The pet pig snuffled for snacks. The dog dashed up, down and all around. And the cat chased the rabbit that zipped and zoomed around the room.

"There's just NO ROOM!" Mom shouted. "Not even for one little piggy!"

"Little piggy, little piggy!" squawked the parrot.

With all the ruckus, Grandma's friends didn't talk much about their book, but they didn't care. They loved being part of Mia's plan.

Once the snacks were eaten, the
apartment emptied out. Sophie came
for Sprinkles. Grandma's neighbor
came for Tigger, Mrs. McGillicuddy
for Pierre. The book club and pet
pig went home. And Grandma
and Roger returned to their freshly
painted apartment.

Mia's mom plopped onto the sofa. "It's funny," she said, "but now our apartment doesn't feel so small anymore."

"Does that mean we can keep Spot?" asked Mia. "He hardly takes up any room."

Mom looked Mia right in the eye ... and winked!
"As long as there are no parrots, rabbits, cats, other
dogs or pigs running around, I think we have room
for one pint-sized pup, after all."